# Sam's
# *Magic Moment*

## Wendy Graham

### Illustrated by Rachel Tonkin

**Rigby**

# Contents

# CHAPTER ONE

# Step Right Up!

"Step right up! Step right up!"

Sam paused. The other noises of the fair faded into the background.

"Ladies and gentlemen! Step right up to see the wonderful, the amazing, the spectacular Marco the Magician!"

Sam caught a glimpse of the man in the purple cape and tall top hat. He was in front of a show tent, standing on a stage.

"He will a-maze you, de-light you, be-dazzle you!"

Quickly, Sam walked the opposite way, without looking back at the magician.

When he was a little boy, Sam thought having a magician for a father was fantastic. He loved that wonderful cape with its hidden treasures, the quick hand movements that tricked the eye, the flick of the wrist that magically produced an egg or a special coin—even a white dove!

Now, it was total embarrassment.

Not that he wished his father was an astronaut or a brain surgeon or a rocket scientist. Something ordinary would do—a cabdriver or a lawyer— like other kids' dads. Practically anything would do—except a magician.

So, Sam had kept his father's occupation a secret, even from his

new best friend Connor. Sam was
afraid Connor would make fun of
him.

# CHAPTER TWO

# The Fair

Sam's eyes scanned the crowds at the fair, looking for Connor. It had been hard for Sam to keep the truth from his friend. It was even more difficult at an event like this where Marco the Magician—Sam's dad—was performing.

He saw Connor and ran over to him. "Hi," Sam said. "The fair's pretty good, isn't it?"

"Yes, it's great."

They bought ice cream cones and wandered around.

"Oh, look. There's a dunk tank!"

They lined up. "Okay, here goes!" called Sam, as he threw the ball. It was a perfect shot.

The seat dropped, and the man sitting in it fell into the water. He came up sputtering, making the boys laugh. They waved goodbye as they walked away.

"Oh, wow, look at that!"

Sam looked to see what Connor was pointing at. The bumper cars! The boys rushed over and handed over their tickets.

When they were both strapped into a small car, they pressed on the pedals and raced around the ring. Sam's car hit the bumpers at the side of the ring, then Connor's car hit Sam's.

The steering wheels weren't much use! The cars seemed to have minds of their own. The boys went around the ring again, laughing.

Finally, their throats sore from shrieking, they climbed out.

"My legs are all wobbly," said Sam.

"Mine, too," said Connor. "Like jelly. Hey, let's play ringtoss!"

Sam agreed to go wherever Connor suggested—except for the show tents. He made sure they didn't go anywhere near Marco the Magician.

# CHAPTER THREE

# That Night

At home that night, Sam's dad made spaghetti, and they sat together at the dinner table.

"Well, Sam, what did you think of the fair today?" his dad asked. Knotted scarves trailed across the room. He had been tying together squares of bright silk—red, blue, and yellow.

"It was good," said Sam. "The bumper cars were so cool."

"Did you find the show tent?" his dad asked. "I didn't see you."

"No, I didn't go there. After I met Connor, we mostly went on rides." Sam didn't meet his father's eyes.

"I've been practicing a new card trick," his dad said. "Want to see?"

Sam finished a mouthful. "Some other time, Dad," he said. "I've got things to do."

After dinner, Sam helped clear the table and went to his room.

His father was thoughtful. What a puzzle. He wished he knew what was wrong with young Salvatore—or Sam, as he liked to be called.

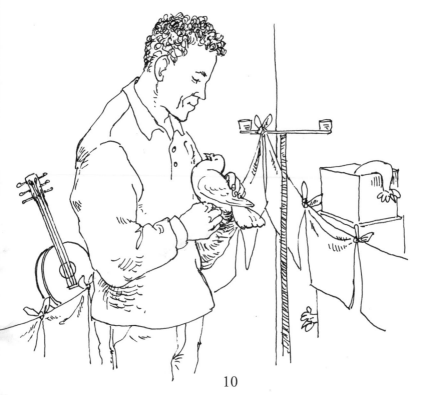

He picked up his old mandolin and tuned the strings. Then he began to strum a tune—an old tune from a place and time far away.

A white dove named Angel cooed from the stand in the corner. Soon, he put the mandolin down and took the bird on his hand. He whistled softly to it, stroking its wing. "You'd like to see my new trick, wouldn't you, Angel?" he asked. He set the bird on the table.

Then he spread out his playing cards. If he perfected this new trick, Marco the Magician might get a job performing at the opening of the new Atlantic Plaza Entertainment Center. That would make his son proud.

# CHAPTER FOUR

# An Ordinary Job

In his room, Sam worked on a model of a rocket. He glued the nose cone and fitted it on. While he waited for the glue to dry, he thought about everything that was bothering him.

He thought about why he'd avoided bringing his friend Connor home. It was because Connor might see his dad rehearsing, dressed in his silly costume. It was because Dad would tweak Connor's ear and produce a shiny coin from behind it, or he would secretly remove Connor's watch and then surprise him by returning it.

Not only that, the props were lying around all over the house where Connor would see them. What ordinary dad has skinny rubber chickens, black boxes with mirrors, heaps of colored handkerchiefs knotted together, and a silly old rope that glues itself back together?

Sam decided to tell his dad the truth. Now!

On the way downstairs, he began silently practicing what he'd say. "Dad, could you try and get an ordinary job? Could you not be a magician any-more?"

He *would* say it, he *would*.

He found his father rehearsing in the living room wearing a cape and a tall top hat. Special music was play-ing from an old cassette player. Sam's dad swirled the cape dramatically as he turned. When he saw Sam, his face lit up. "Salvatore! You've come to see my new trick. I'll start again."

Sam sighed. He sat and watched his father's performance. It was pretty good, actually. He didn't say the things he'd planned. How could he?

# CHAPTER FIVE

# Aunt Rosa

Sam's dad was getting ready to go out.

"I'm too old for a baby-sitter," Sam protested.

"Aunt Rosa is not a baby-sitter," his father said. "She's just spending time with you while I audition for the Atlantic Plaza opening."

"It's still baby-sitting."

"Now, Salvatore, don't be difficult. Help me pack the car. You bring Angel and my props case. Where's my magic wand?"

Sam groaned. Nothing would ever change.

When Aunt Rosa came, Sam tried to tell her how he felt. "I wish Dad had a different job, Aunt Rosa," he said, "instead of being a magician."

"Oh, Sam," said Aunt Rosa. "Your dad has always loved magic."

"Why can't he have an ordinary job?" Then Sam added, "Like other dads."

Aunt Rosa looked at him. "He had an ordinary job in the old country," she said. "He sold vegetables, which he loved. Here, in the city, he can't grow enough vegetables to sell."

Sam sighed and Aunt Rosa's face became serious. "He did have a job in the city. When your mother went away, he could not work. He stayed at home to look after you!"

Sam nodded. "Couldn't he find an ordinary job now? I'm not little anymore."

Aunt Rosa shook her head. "He tried," she said, "but he had no luck. It gave him much sadness. Now he makes a good living from magic—and he loves it. To love what you do is very important."

Sam understood, but he still wished his dad wasn't a magician. It was hard keeping it a secret from Connor.

# CHAPTER SIX

# Juggling Pineapples

Dad came home from the audition.

"Hello, Rosa. Hello, Sam," he called. "Guess what?" He twirled around the room, swishing his cape over his shoulder. "I will be performing in Atlantic Plaza's main parade and for their grand opening week, too! I will have a big stage with a spotlight and a live band! What do you think of that?"

From his cape, he produced a tube. With a sweeping motion, he threw a shower of fluorescent sparkles that settled on the walls and floor in a patterned arc. He clasped his hands together. "Ah, *bellissima*, yes? Beautiful." The sparkles blazed for a moment before disappearing.

Then he went into his introduction. "Marco the Magician will a-maze you, de-light you, be-dazzle you."

He gave Sam a bear hug. "You'll come, won't you? It's in two weeks."

Sam's heart sank.

The next day, Connor invited Sam to his house after school. It was raining, so they couldn't play outside. Sam looked through a pile of CDs.

"We can't play music," said Connor. "My dad's an architect and he works from home. He can't have any noise in the house."

Connor switched on the computer. "We can play computer games if you want. I've got a new one."

"Oh, great," said Sam.

"But it has to be with the sound turned off," added Connor.

They played the new computer game, but it wasn't as much fun without the sound effects.

"Why don't we go back to your house?" suggested Connor. "Can't we be noisy there?"

Sam knew that at his house they could make as much noise as they wanted.

But then he pictured his dad rehearsing in his magician's cape, which he needed to wear for practice because it held his props. Even if he wore ordinary clothes, he'd probably be juggling pineapples or something.

What would Connor do? He'd probably laugh!

"No," Sam said. "Maybe some other time."

# CHAPTER SEVEN

# The Big Parade

Crowds lined the street. A big parade was being held to celebrate the opening of Atlantic Plaza, the new entertainment center. Television cameras were filming the parade, which had just begun.

Sam and Connor found themselves a good place to stand in the crowd.

The musicians began to play marching music. Then the floats started down the street. Between the floats there were costumed dancers, marching girls twirling batons, acrobats doing cartwheels, and clowns juggling balls.

Along came a horse-drawn cart full of waving children. Right behind the cart was Sam's dad. Wearing his magician's outfit, he rode an old-fashioned bicycle. He waved to the crowds with both hands, a broad grin on his face.

CRACK! A sudden loud shot from a toy cannon on one of the floats made everyone jump. The horses bolted. The children in the cart screamed as they were taken on a wild ride down the street.

"Help! Somebody help!"

Sam's dad sped up on his bicycle. He leaned forward, riding faster and faster. His top hat flew off. His cape flowed out behind him.

The children in the cart squealed in fright. "Help! Help!" they cried, clinging desperately to the cart.

Sam's dad pedaled furiously and came up alongside the horses. He leaped from the bike, landed on the back of one horse, and grabbed the reins. With the horse galloping beneath him, he held on with one hand and reached toward the other horse. Then he pulled both frightened animals to a stop.

A wild cheer broke out in the crowd. Some people clapped. Sam's dad helped the children from the wagon. A police officer came and patted him on the back.

"That was great!" she said.

# CHAPTER EIGHT

# You'll See

Afterward, when the excitement had passed and the parade was over, Sam went back to Connor's house. Sam's dad had to rehearse for his magic show that evening.

Connor's mother gave the boys a bowl of popcorn. The news was on TV.

Sam's eyes widened as he saw the parade, the bolting horses, and Marco the Magician chasing the horses with the cart full of children.

"Wow, look at that!" said Connor.

"Shh, listen," said Connor's mother. "They're interviewing that brave man."

Sam stared at the television. The reporter was speaking to his father. Now he was dressed in ordinary clothes. He looked uncomfortable in front of the camera.

"Have you ever ridden a horse before?" the reporter asked.

"Never."

"It was the bravest thing I've seen for a long time. You're a hero!" the reporter exclaimed.

Sam's dad shook his head. "No, no. I am just an ordinary man," he said. "Most of all . . ." he paused, and his gentle smile filled the television screen, "most of all, I am a father to the best son in the world."

Sam's heart sang. A commercial came on and Connor's mother poured the boys a glass of juice.

Sam suddenly made a decision.

"Connor," he said, "my dad's performing all this week at Atlantic Plaza. Will you come with me and see the show?"

Connor finished his juice. "Okay," he said. "What does your dad do?"

"You'll see," said Sam.

# CHAPTER NINE

# My Dad, the Magician

Aunt Rosa led the boys to the front-row seats. The stage was empty, the lights dim.

"Ladies and gentlemen," said a booming voice. "He will a-maze you, de-light you, be-dazzle you! Introducing the incredible, the spectacular—Marco the Magician!"

The band began to play and Sam's dad strode onto the stage, swishing his black cape. The crowd applauded.

Connor, looking at the band members, nudged Sam. "Which one is your dad?"

"He's not in the band," Sam answered. "My dad's the magician."

"Wow!" Connor said.

Marco the Magician snapped his fingers and Angel, the dove, flew to him. He waved a red silk handkerchief and Angel disappeared. He pretended to search for the dove, showing she was not inside his cape. Then he bowed and took off his top hat—and there was Angel inside!

The crowd applauded—Sam, Connor, and Aunt Rosa most of all.

The show continued. It was true—Marco the Magician did amaze, delight, and bedazzle them. He was the best he had ever been.

At intermission, they went to his dressing room and Sam introduced Connor.

"The trick with the dove?" Connor asked. "How did you do that?"

Sam's dad tweaked Connor's ear and from behind it, to Connor's surprise, he produced a tiny toy racing car.

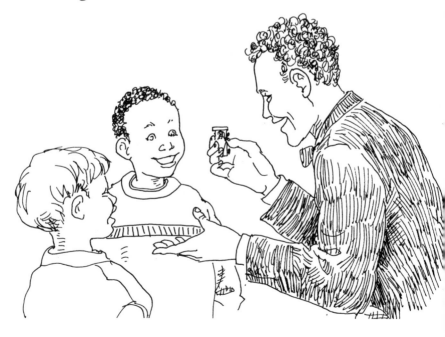

"A magician never tells his secrets," Marco the Magician said, smiling.

When the boys went back to their seats for the rest of the show, Connor turned to Sam. "You've got a cool dad," he said.

Sam was nearly bursting with pride. "I know," he said.